DOODLES

Written and illustrated by
Zack Giallongo

EGMONT
We bring stories to life

First published in Great Britain 2015
by Egmont UK Limited, The Yellow Building,
1 Nicholas Road, London W11 4AN.

ISBN 978 1 4052 7636 8
59021/4
Printed in Italy

To find more great *Star Wars* books, visit www.egmont.co.uk/starwars

Use circles to draw Tatooine's twin suns
— or however many suns you want!

Whoa! The Sand People want to build an awesome sand castle. Help them out!

One of the stormtroopers crashed Darth Vader's ship and he has to use one of the replacements. Will you draw it for him?

Draw the alien that took Han Solo's seat at the cantina when Han got up to get a drink.

What strange gadget did Chewie find on the *Millennium Falcon*?

2-1B lost Luke's new hand and is trying a few different options.

Draw some coral for Admiral Ackbar
to swim through.

He looks so happy!

Draw Leia's new hairstyle!

And Yoda's!

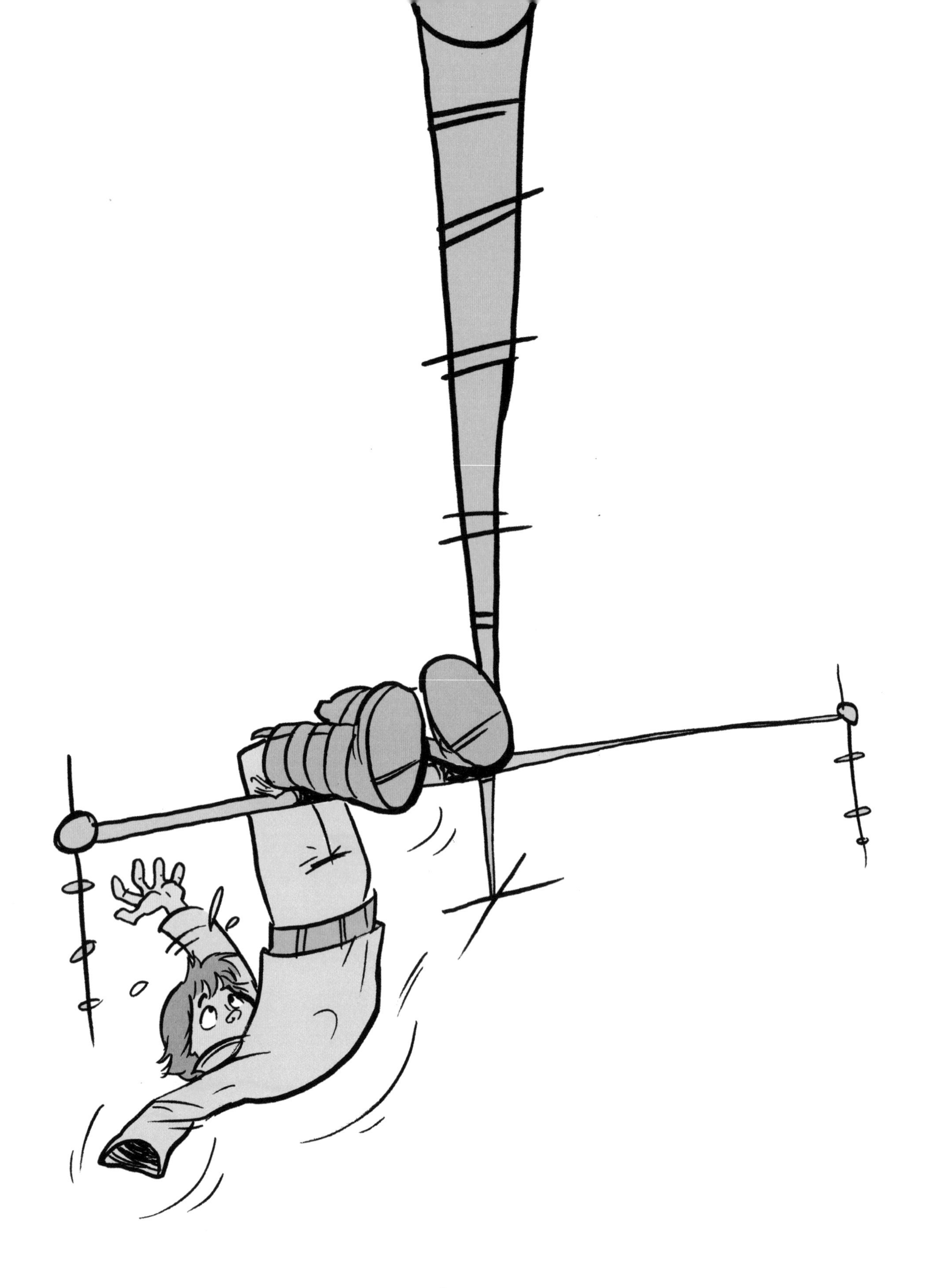

Who is hanging out with
Luke under Cloud City?

Use zigzags to draw
Lando's moustache.

The Ewoks are getting new hoods! What do they look like?

Don't forget to add some bones!

What does the inside of the Sarlacc pit look like?
Is it scary?
Or cosy?

What does a Jawa look like
under its hood?

Darth Vader and Boba Fett are chatting with their new honoured guest!

Who is joining them for dinner?

Who's angry with Lando this time?

"What does the Force look like, Master Yoda?"

"Invisible, it is!"

Luke's not so sure.

Draw what appears out of the swamp.

Use zigzags to draw Palpatine's Force lightning!

"MUAHAHAHAHA!"

Oh, no! Draw an asteroid field!

Finish drawing this droid. Make him cool.

Jabba wants you to draw a tattoo for him.

Draw the Royal Guard's feet!

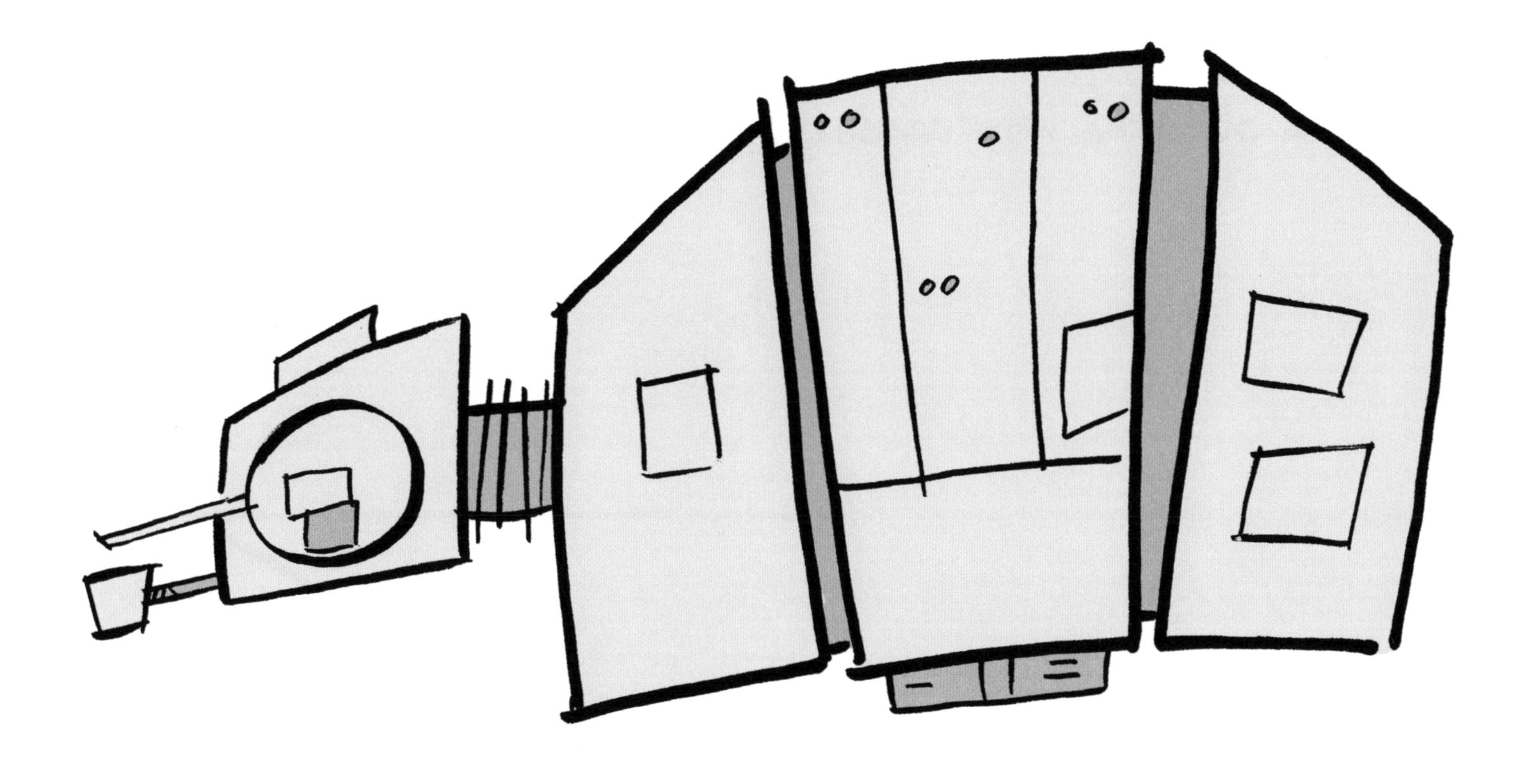

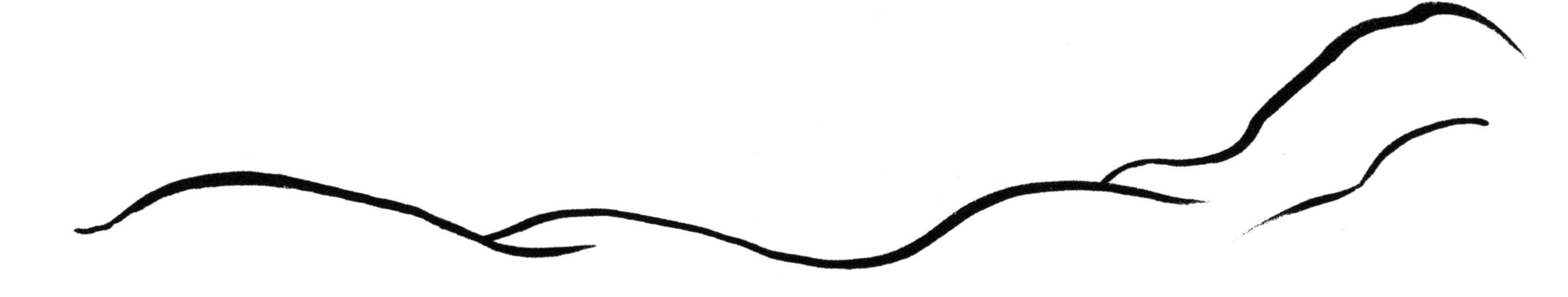

This AT-AT can't walk if it doesn't have legs.
Draw some!

Check out the new dancer at Jabba's palace!

Dress up the droids!

Give Han Solo
a disguise.

Use Xs to make a whole fleet of X-wings.
Now add some cool details.
Don't forget to draw Red Leader!

Use rectangles and circles to add to the Lars homestead.

Luke is surprised by what's under Darth Vader's helmet.

Han thought the tauntaun smelled bad on the outside! Use lots of squiggles in this drawing!

Draw lines and circles to show the *Millennium Falcon* blasting through hyperspace!

R2-D2 just got a bunch of new attachments. Draw them!

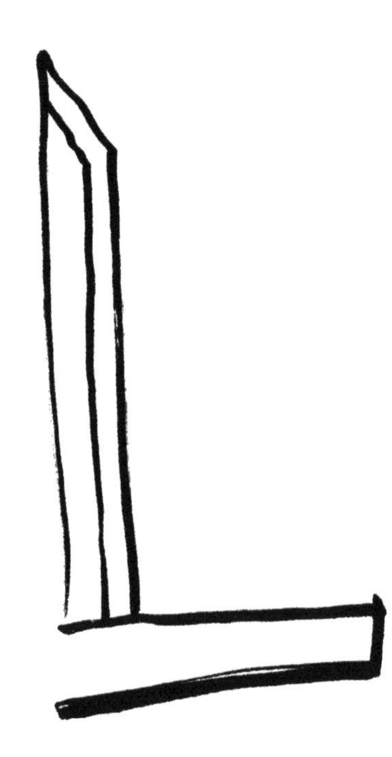

What are Luke and Leia swinging over?

Draw the stormtroopers' blaster fire!
PEW!
PEW!
PEW!
PEW!

Obi-Wan does a pretty good krayt dragon impression to scare away the Sand People. Draw lines to show him shouting!

Draw some fire coming out of Boba Fett's jet pack!

Draw lines and squiggles to show Luke wrapped up in Boba Fett's trap!

Decorate this stormtrooper's helmet any way you like!

Meet the new server at the cantina!

Draw Obi-Wan Kenobi's beard.

BEEP-BOOP-BEEP!

Who is hiding in the snow from the Imperial probe droid?

What does a dianoga look like beneath all the water, sludge and trash?

Draw upside-down Vs to make the Gamorreans' armour spikier and more awesome!

Add squiggles to make the Ewoks' bonfire.

Darth Vader's TIE fighter needs wings!

Draw the coolest wings ever.

R2-D2 has an important message
from someone! What is it?

Look what Leia found while brushing Chewbacca's fur!

Grand Moff Tarkin is sporting a very fancy moustache these days, don't you think?

Jabba's about to eat something gross!

Luke is practising using the Force.

Draw circles to make training remotes.

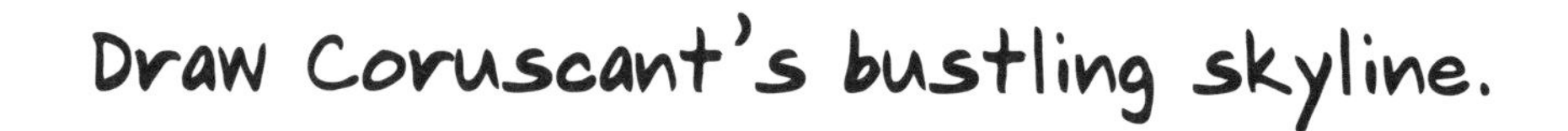
Draw Coruscant's bustling skyline.

Chewie didn't receive his
medal at the Battle of Yavin.
Draw one to cheer him up!

Quick! Help Lando disguise himself
from Jabba's henchmen!

Who is frozen in this slab of carbonite?

What do you think of C-3PO's new body?

What did Yoda lift out of
the swamp with the Force?

Hello, what have we here?

Help Lando decorate his cape!

Max Rebo just got
new instruments
for the band!

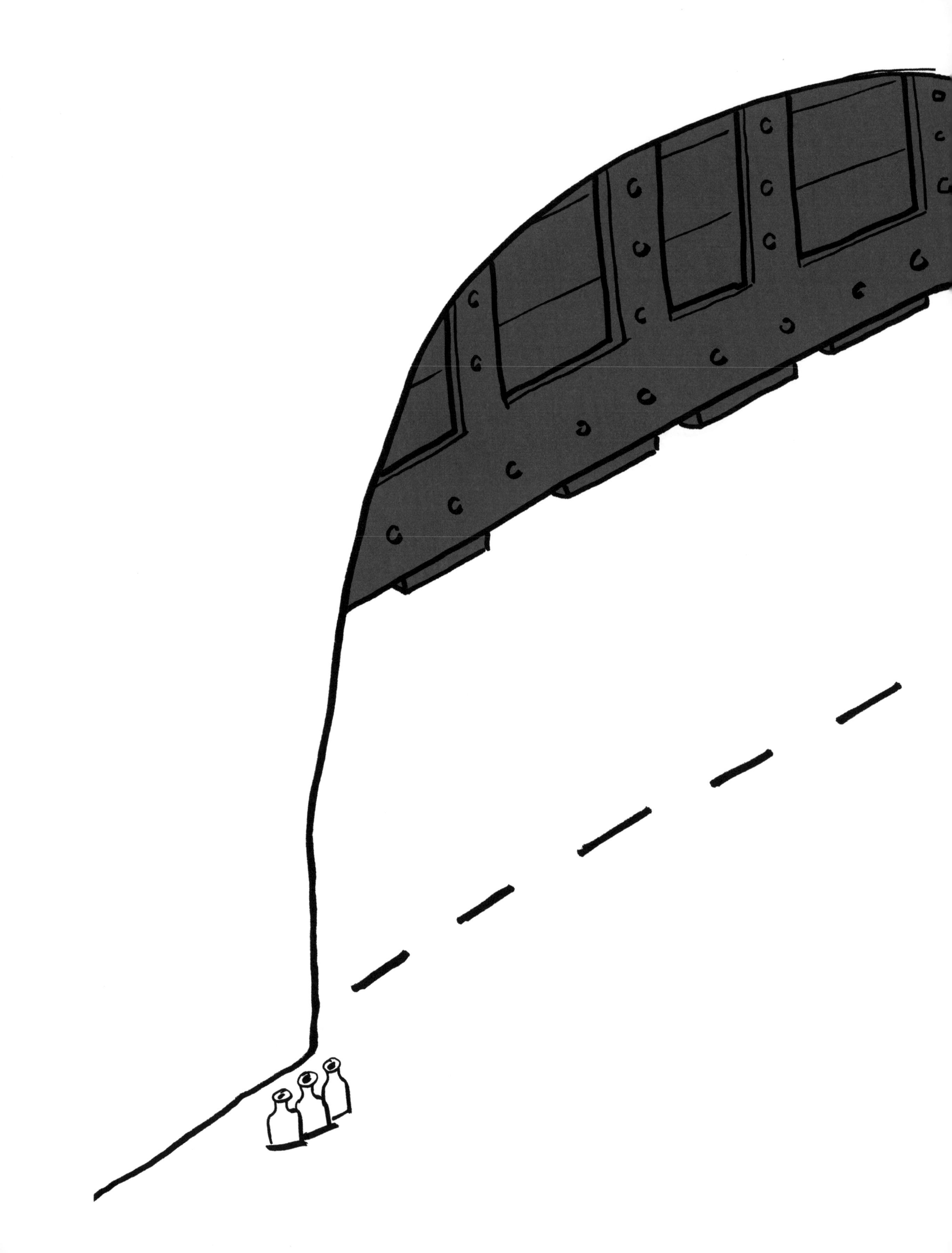

Draw whoever is answering the door at Jabba's palace ...

and draw a welcome mat.

Make holochess characters
that will help Chewie win.

Use circles and squares to draw Darth Vader's new chest plate.

This Imperial console needs buttons, knobs, monitors and levers.

An air guitar is not enough for Mon Mothma.

Draw her a real one so she can join Max Rebo's band!

It's about time Lobot had some hair.

Put some cool sunglasses on everyone, and don't forget to trick out the landspeeder!

What do you think is in Yoda's stew?

Draw some things for Luke to practise levitating with the Force.

Something huge is trying to eat the *Millennium Falcon*!

What (or who) did the Ewoks catch in their net this time?

Draw the Sarlacc's tentacles ...
and its lunch!

Give this stormtrooper some way-cool armour modifications.

Two banthas are missing their horns.

Draw curly lines to add them.

Draw lines to show how fast the speeder bikes are going!

VROOOOM!

Now you can draw the other half of Lord Vader's helmet! How lucky are you?

What are these bounty hunters snacking on during their break?

Now that Luke Skywalker is a Jedi, he wants some cool sideburns.

Draw the treetops of Endor while Darth Vader and Luke have a father-son chat.

>GONK< Draw squares to finish this power droid. >GONK<

Draw squiggles and zigzags to show the Jawa zapping R2!

Have R2 zap him right back!

It's swampy!

Draw the vegetation and rain around Yoda's hut on Dagobah.

Show an X-wing pilot being ejected!

Nien Nunb needs ears!

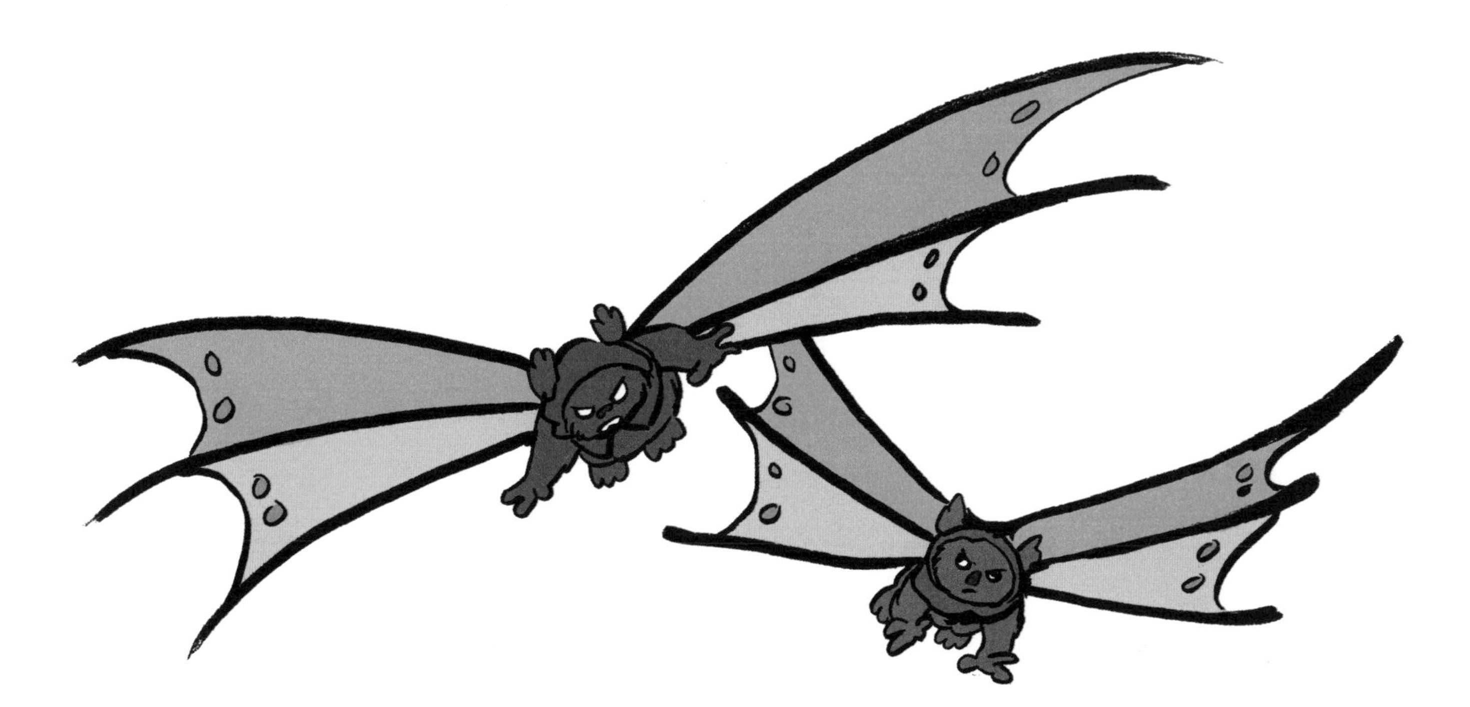

Draw what the Ewoks are dropping onto the stormtroopers below!

These guys aren't too sure about
the new Imperial commander.

Who is under this hood?

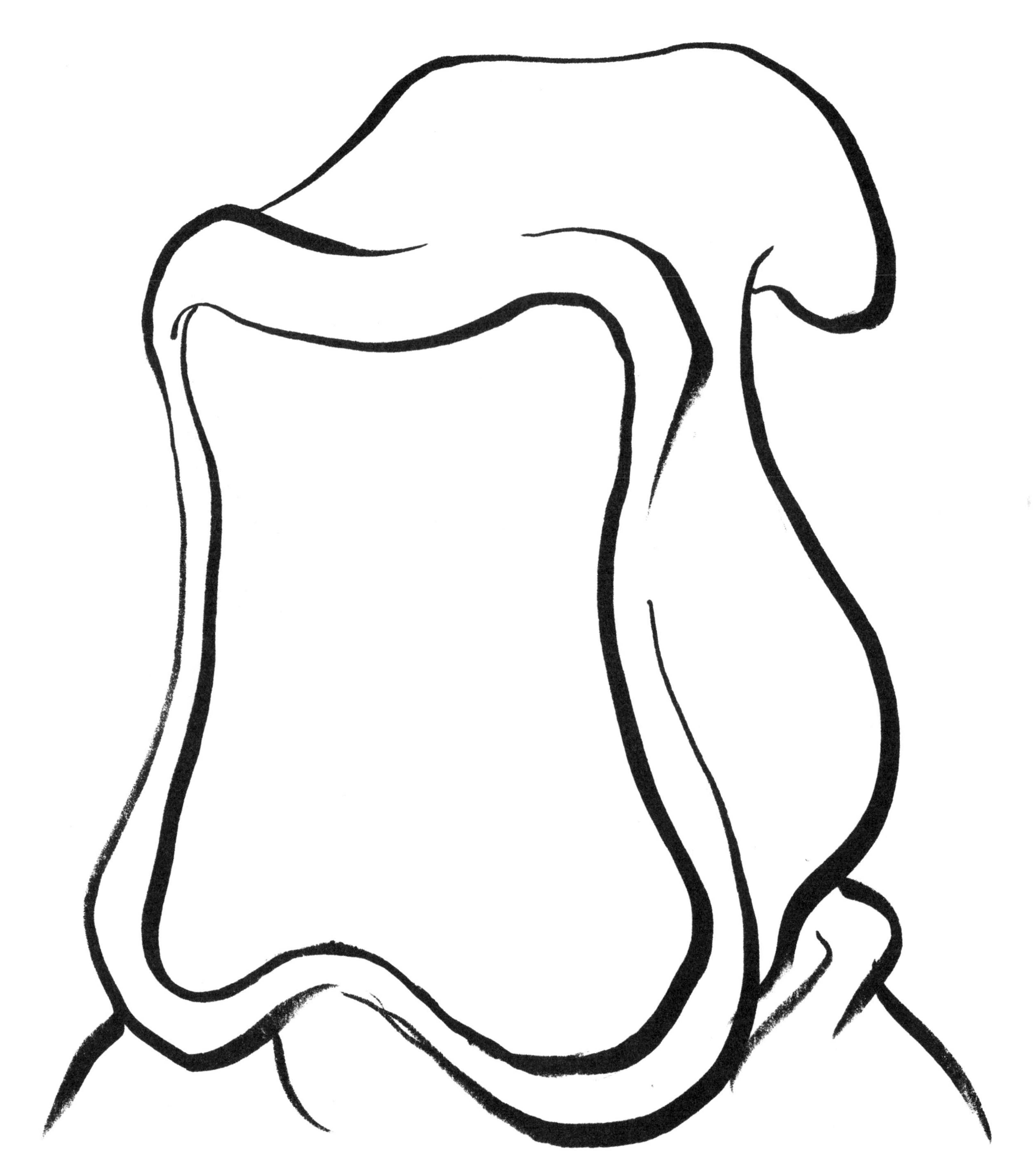

Who does that vile gangster Jabba the Hutt have in his dungeon cell?

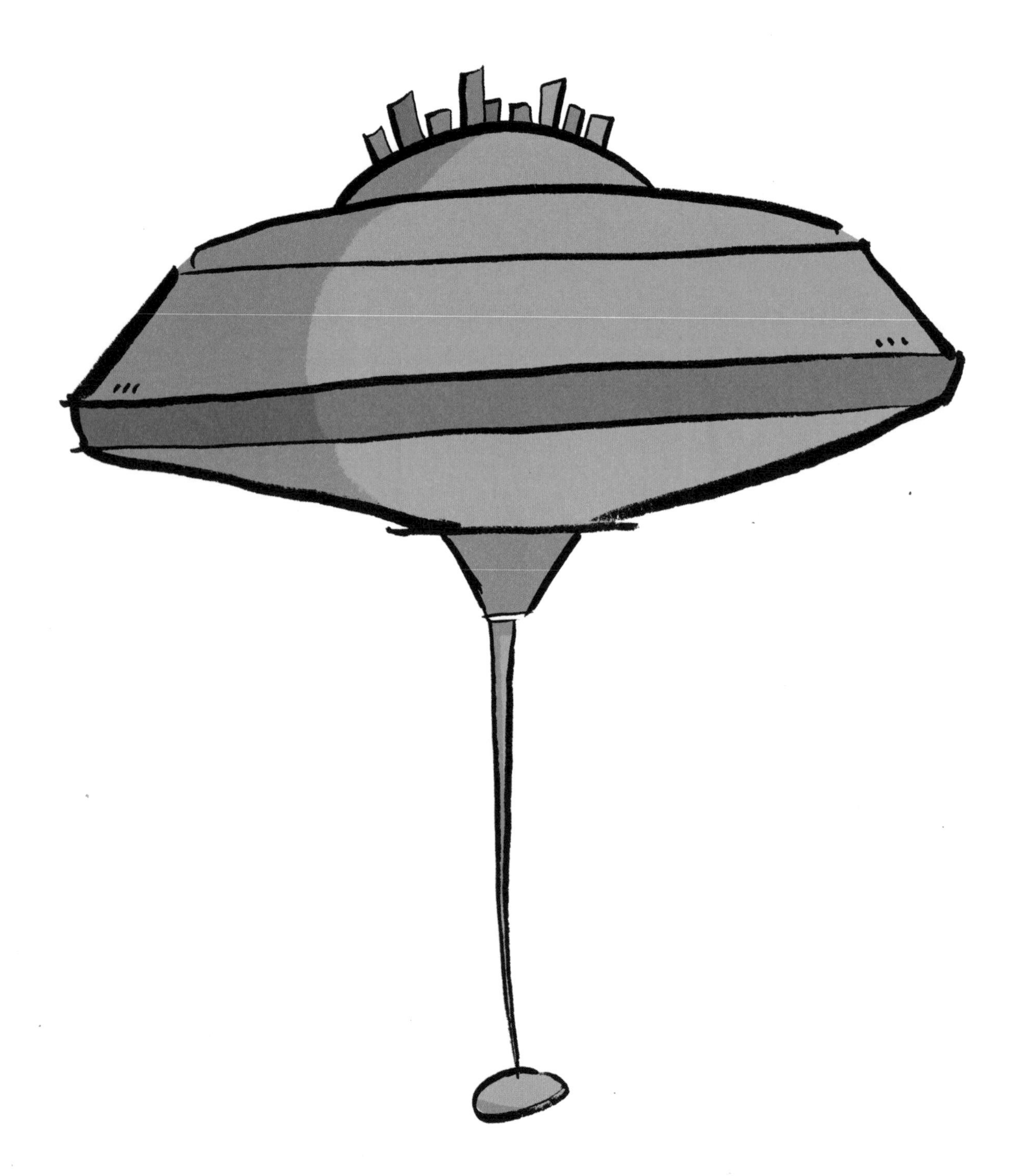

Fill Cloud City with clouds and starships.

It's breakfast time for Greedo.

Drat! Luke misplaced his lightsaber. Draw him something else to use to battle the Dark Lord of the Sith!

Add fur to Han's hood and his tauntaun.

Blast! The *Millennium Falcon* is broken again.

Draw tools for Han and Chewie to fix it with.

Give Tarkin a cool pair of boots.

Draw lines to make a bridge for Obi-Wan to walk across to disable the Death Star's tractor beam.

Luke and Biggs find many womp rats in Beggar's Canyon.

Draw more of these vicious creatures.

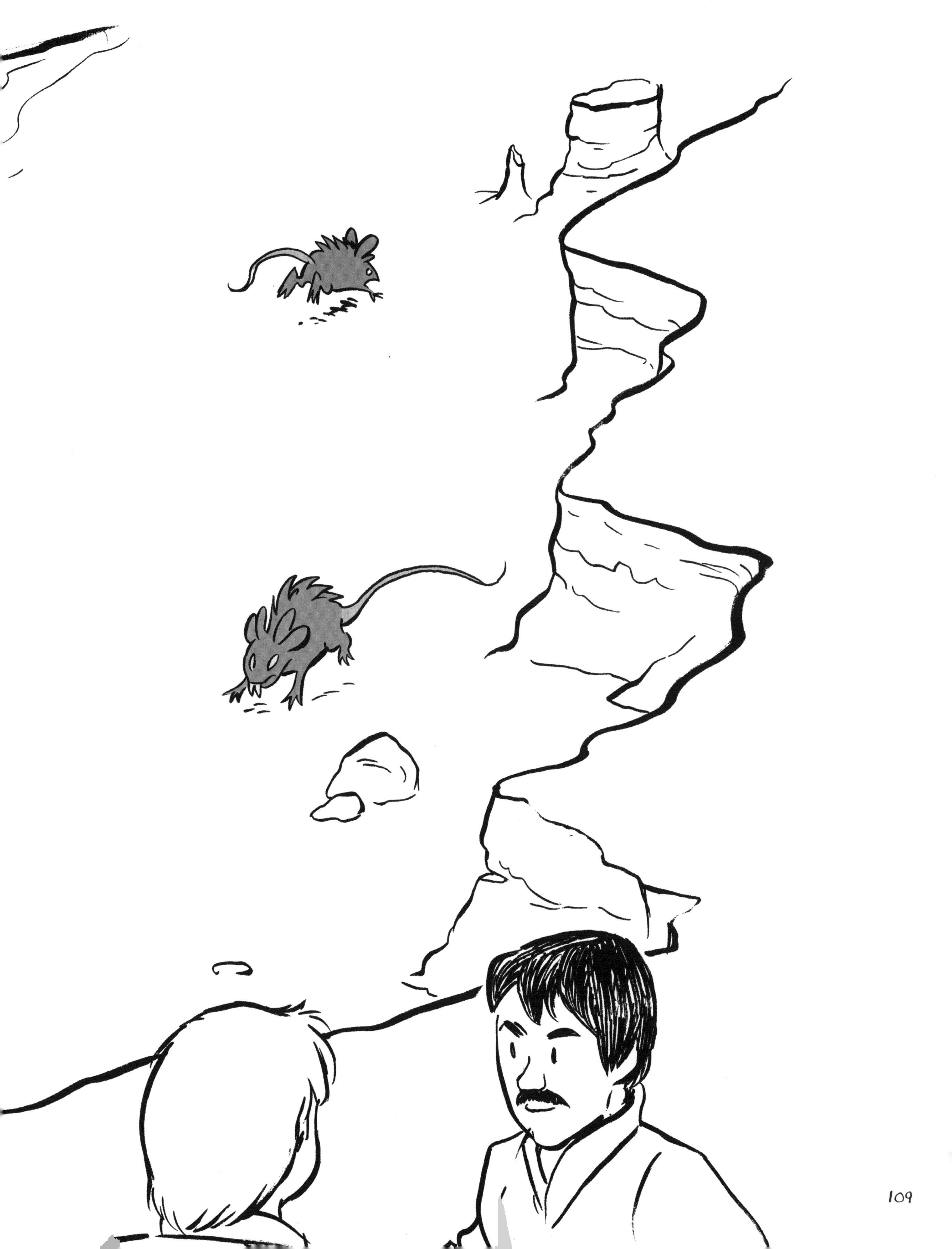

What did Vader find in Obi-Wan's pockets?

Who is that
dressed up as
the bounty hunter
Boushh?

Draw the torpedo hurtling towards the ventilation shaft!

Draw traps for Ackbar to avoid!

These Sand People need something to wave while shouting.

Draw blaster fire for Luke to deflect!

Fill this whole scene with stars.

Who is Han talking to?

Draw some surf and sun
for Bossk to bask in.

What is that foul stench?

And who does Tarkin have at
the end of his leash?

Who is Garindan spying
on in Mos Eisley?

Draw a battle of the bands!

Happy birthday, Boba! What is his present?

Disgusting creatures!

What did the Jawas find in the landspeeder this time?

Luke needs to clean and polish R2 and C-3PO.
Show how beat up and dirty they are.

Put some cool decorations and insignia on this pilot's helmet.

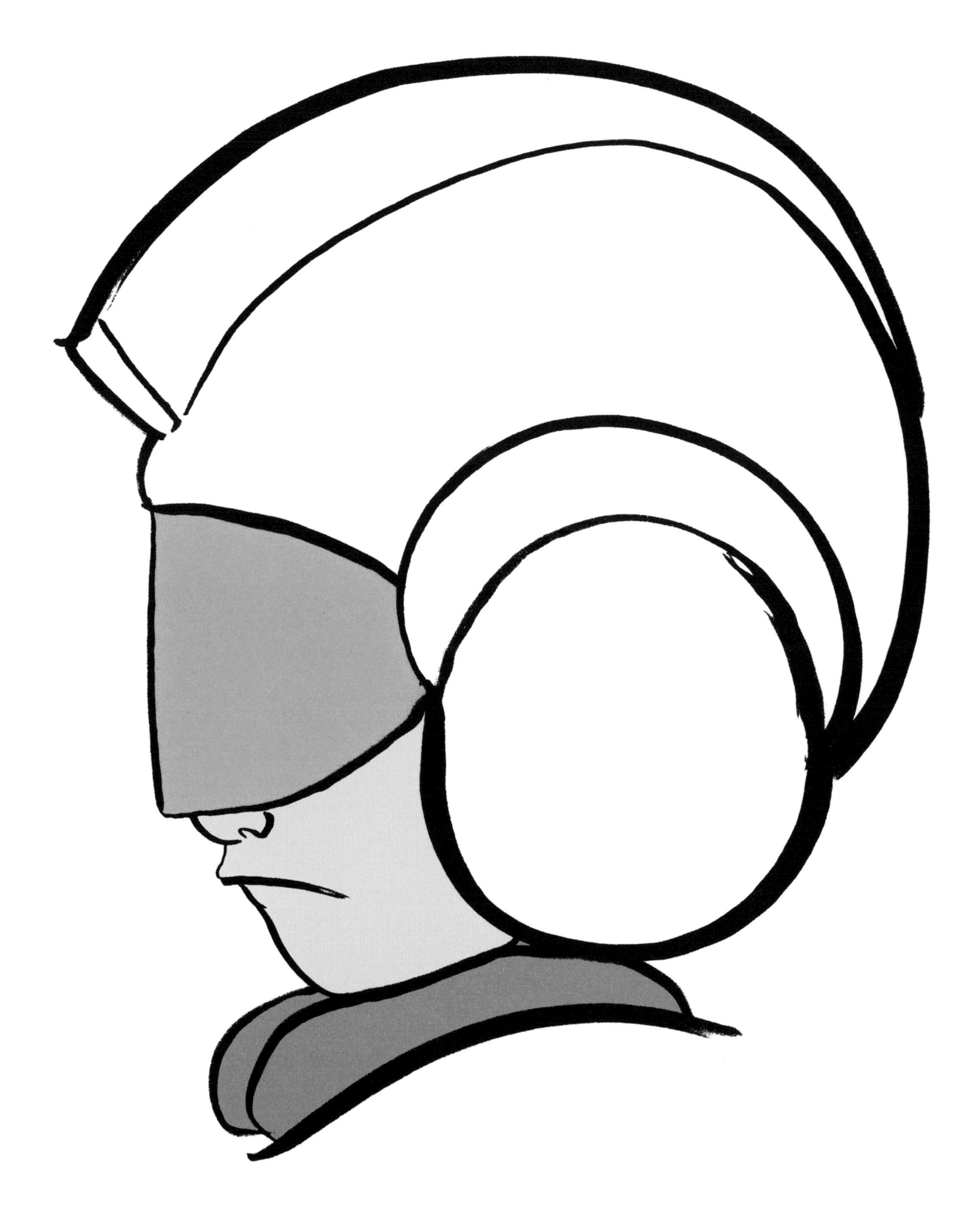

Draw the Death Star blowing up.
BOOM!